Just Like Daddy

FRANK ASCH

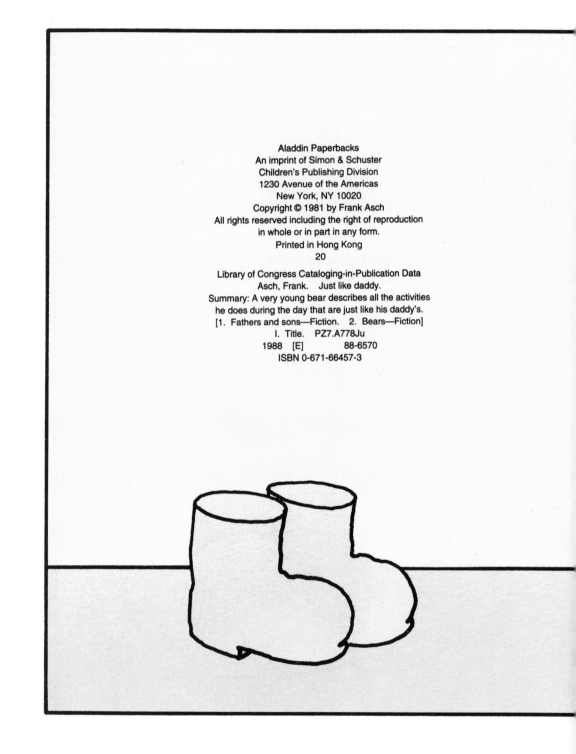

Aladdin Paperbacks
An imprint of Simon & Schuster
Children's Publishing Division
1230 Avenue of the Americas
New York, NY 10020
Copyright © 1981 by Frank Asch
Printed in Hong Kong
20
Library of Congress Cataloging-in-Publication Data
Asch, Frank.   Just like daddy.
Summary: A very young bear describes all the activities
he does during the day that are just like his daddy's.
[1. Fathers and sons—Fiction.   2. Bears—Fiction]
I. Title.   PZ7.A778Ju
1988   [E]   88-6570
ISBN 0-671-66457-3

To Devin

When I got up this morning
I yawned a big yawn…

Just like Daddy.

I washed my face, got dressed,
and had a big breakfast…

Just like Daddy.

Then I put on my coat
and my boots…

Just like Daddy.

And we all went fishing.

On the way I picked a flower
and gave it to my mother…

Just like Daddy.

When we got to the lake,
I put a big worm on my hook…

Just like Daddy.

All day we fished and fished,
and I caught a big fish...

Just like Mommy!